KNOCKOUT

A BBW & BAD BOY ROMANCE

LANA LOVE

LOVE HEART BOOKS

Copyright © 2023 by Lana Love

All rights reserved.

No part of this book may be reproduced in any form or by any electronic or mechanical means, including information storage and retrieval systems, without written permission from the author, except for the use of brief quotations in a book review.

For more books by Lana Love, please visit:

https://www.loveheartbooks.com

❀ Created with Vellum

CHAPTER 1

SHELLY

"I'm not sure about this." I stand outside Champ's Gym, debating whether I should turn around and go home. Luann would be disappointed, but…it's Tuesday afternoon, and this isn't how I want to spend my day off work. I'm not even sure I'm strong enough to do this. Coming this far has been a huge deal for me.

"You're going to be fine, Shelly. I promise." Luann's voice is patient, though she can never quite hide her exasperation.

It's not like I wanted an abusive boyfriend, but no matter how much I wish for it, putting him in the past isn't as easy as snapping my fingers.

"You said Caleb would be here, right?" I'll probably never understand why she let herself fall in love with a man who thinks it's fun to hit other people, but I'm certainly no pro when it comes to dating or love, so I keep my mouth shut. It's not like I can talk after what my ex, Larry, put me through. He thought because I'm overweight, that I'm desperate and would accept any attention he'd give me. The sad part was, that was true.

Now, I believe I'm worth more, but the hard part is making the changes needed.

I rub the tenderness at the top of my arm, wincing at the reminder of how he took it when I said we were over.

"Yes, he's there if you need him." The sound of the hospital comes through the phone. She's determined to work as late in her pregnancy as possible, but the hospital pulled her from the ER rotation. "Shelly, I've met Floyd. He's a good man. He's quiet, so don't read too much into that. I trust him completely. If Caleb vouches for him–and he has–you'll be in good hands. You can trust him, I swear."

I wince, though I believe her.

I still can't believe she's married now, much less pregnant. Luann! Everyone assumed I'd be the one having kids, not Luann. These days, I don't know if I want kids. I don't trust men, and the thought of being connected to a man for the rest of my life scares the shit out of me.

Luann laughs, and I hear another nurse calling her name. "He knows he has nothing to worry about, Shelly. Nothing at all. You're not one to be single for long, and that gym has no shortage of hot men."

"Don't set me up just yet. You know how I feel about fighting. Besides, I need to be on my own for a while."

"True, but you're still a hot-blooded woman." The sounds on the phone muffle, and I hear her calling out to one of her colleagues. "Look, I have to go. Call me when you're done, and remember, Caleb is there. If you freak out, find him or

Champ, and they'll take care of you. I'm proud of you for doing this, Shelly. Love you."

I take a deep breath as I glance at the sign above the door.

Of all the places I never thought I'd be... Maybe I'll learn how to protect myself.

I don't kid myself. Even if I did learn how to defend myself, I'm not sure I'd be able to fight if I were cornered. The idea of hitting someone makes my skin crawl, but...I'm done with being pushed around. I'm especially done with Larry thinking he can come around any old time he wants and hit me if he's drunk or decides I've done something wrong. He forgets that I threw him out three months ago. Every time he returns from driving his rig, like he did last week, he shows up at my door, trying to romance or threaten me into giving him what he wants.

"Hey. You okay out here?"

I startle at the voice and turn to see a muscular man several years older than me, which puts him close to forty. I must look scared because he takes a step back and holds up his hands. Is my pain that obvious?

"Um... My sister told me about a self-defense class?" The trembling in my voice is unmistakable.

The man's expression softens. "You Luann's sister? She said you'd be coming by. This is my place. I'm Champ." He smiles at me warmly, and some of my hesitation melts away. He doesn't look scary.

"Oh! Luann told me about you." I stumble over my words, sure I'm making a fool of myself.

One night over dinner, Caleb told Luann and me how Champ was a pro boxer for a while after getting out of the Army. He's always been a father figure to other fighters, so he opened his own gym.

"The good things are lies, and the bad things are probably true." Champ smiles at me, and the tension in my shoulders lessens. "Floyd is running late, but come in with me and I'll show you around."

Champ pushes open a heavy front door, letting bright sunlight into the large gym. Men are boxing or sparring everywhere I look, and the musky smell of men is unavoidable. I follow Champ into the gym, folding my arms across my chest as my nerves tingle again. A couple of the men look at me, but their eyes flick to Champ, and they look away. I'm not sure if coming here was a good idea, but I need to learn how to defend myself.

"Hold on a sec and I'll get you some gloves." Champ disappears into a cluttered office and leaves me standing at the side of the gym.

My heart races as I look around and take in my surroundings. My sister has been at me for months to take a self-defense class here, even going so far as to say she'd arrange a private class with one of the boxers. It's been hard to get to this point because it meant kicking Larry out of my life once and for all. He didn't think I was serious when I told him it was over, but I realized that if *I* didn't change, I'd be miserable forever. Larry would've stayed with me for as long as I'd let him, and also that he'd hit me for just as long.

When Luann found love with Caleb, it was proof that true love exists. It reminded me of what real, healthy love looks like. Seeing how Caleb stepped up when he found out she was pregnant and how he's proven himself to be an excellent man made me want the same thing for myself. I want my life back. I want *me* back. Watching them together motivates me to make changes in my life, so I can discover my own happy ending.

I stand with my back against a wall of framed photographs, but I'm focused on the men in the gym. Two men are sparring in a ring, and I try not to wince as one of them takes a blow to the head. He steps back and shakes his arms and body like the blow was insignificant.

I wish it were that easy for me when Larry hit me.

Watching them reminds me why I'm here. Larry keeps reappearing and trying to charm me, even though I have no intention of giving him a second chance.

"I don't even have to ask if you're ready."

My head snaps up at the man's voice. I didn't even notice him approaching me.

"Excuse me?" I snap, a jolt of adrenaline putting all my senses on high alert. I instinctively raise my hands in front of me, trying to create distance between us.

"That came out wrong. I'm Floyd. I'm going to help you learn how to box." The man raises his hands in surrender and takes a step back, which is funny given that he's built like a shithouse, has tattoos, and is nearly a foot taller than me. "I apologize. You do, however, look like you're ready to take on the guys in the ring–both of them–and knock them six ways to Sunday. And judging by your expression…my money's on you."

"Thanks? I guess." I can't tell if he's shitting me or if he's serious. Understanding the difference between what men say and what they mean has never been my strong point, and it's gotten me into trouble. I thought I looked scared, but maybe I looked angry. I wouldn't be surprised.

He looks at me as if he's waiting for me to say something else. "Luann said you'd be coming in and that you wanted to learn how to defend yourself. She asked me to teach you one-on-one." His already-deep voice drops an octave. "She mentioned you were having problems with your boyfriend."

"Ex-boyfriend." The correction leaves my mouth before I realize I'm interrupting him. Every time I say it, I believe it a little more, despite it being scary to be single again.

"This is a safe place. Okay?" Floyd says patiently.

My stomach flip-flops. Something about him makes me feel safe, which is ridiculous since I just met him. He's exactly the kind of man who makes me weak. He's gruff and darkly handsome, with a full sleeve of tattoos on one arm and a lattice of scars on the other. Desire pulls deep inside me and it takes me a moment too long to push it down.

Men like him are precisely how I got into this situation. No, Shelly. No.

I want to learn how to be happy alone, not bounce from one man to the next, but I'm the kind of woman who needs a man in my life. Problem is, I'm lousy at choosing men. So as much as I hate being single, I know it's for the best right now.

Blinking rapidly, I nod and introduce myself, though the desire won't extinguish itself. Everything has been an emotional rollercoaster this last year, and I need to move past it. It took me a while, but I finally realized Luann was right about learning self-defense. I had to take control of my life instead of hoping Larry would give up and leave me alone.

"Thanks." I remind myself that Floyd is not an enemy and force myself to relax a little. Standing in this gym, I'm a fish out of water. But if I want my life to change, learning how to look out for myself is the first step.

Seemingly satisfied that I'm not going to try and punch him or scream, Floyd nods at me and directs me toward a corner of the gym.

"Okay. Let's get started."

CHAPTER 2

FLOYD

Tension radiates off Shelly. If she bolted out the door and never came back, that would be the least surprising part of my day.

Shelly looks at me for a long moment, then nods.

"Alright. Let's go over to the heavy bags," I say, gesturing toward a corner of the gym. "You can put your stuff down against the wall. I'll get some gloves."

"Champ said he was going to find me some, but he disappeared into the office," I gesture across the gym, "and never came out."

Sighing, I look at the office and see Champ on the phone. "It happens. I'll pick them up, and we'll get started."

I watch as she puts her things down, my eyes lingering on the curve of her wide hips. God bless whoever created yoga pants. Watching her is like a punch to the solar plexus. The fear in her eyes as she looks around the gym is the most powerful thing I've experienced in a long time. Having her come in after hours might have been a better idea, but that can't be helped now.

"Everything okay over there?" Champ asks as he puts down the phone.

He's got a pile of paper next to him and a look on his face that reveals how much he still resents Beth for taking the job at the bank. Between her new job and upcoming wedding to Dirk, she's happy and content, though I wouldn't say that to Champ's face. I don't know anything about business or bookkeeping, but even I can see he needs help–Champ's just too hard-headed to trust a stranger.

"I think it will be. Ask me in an hour. Did you find some gloves for her?" I glance over my shoulder and see her pressing her back against the wall, her arms crossed tightly over her chest. "It's fifty-fifty if she bolts or not."

"Yeah, sorry about that. Got caught by the damn phone. Here you go."

I nod and return to Shelly, who's still standing with her arms wrapped across her chest. I ease up to her, and she lets me help her with the gloves. It's intoxicating to stand close to her, and it knocks me off balance. Something magnetic flows between us, and when her eyes widen as I help her, I know I'm not the only one feeling it.

"Alright. I'm going to take you through some basics. Usually, for self-defense, I'd show you some other things, but from what I understand, you need more, uh…practical lessons."

Shelly's eyes grow dark, but she nods. "It's stupid because I hate violence. But I don't know what else to do."

I admire that she's trying to work her way out of a bad situation and taking steps to protect herself. I had a rough childhood, and the only thing that got me out was believing I could control my future. I didn't want to end up in jail, which is where everyone assumed I'd land. I'm not living a life of luxury, but I've got a steady job, solid friends, and boxing keeps me in shape and lets me blow off steam.

"You're in the right place. I'll teach you everything I know." I breathe a little easier when Shelly starts to relax. I pause as I catch a good look at her t-shirt. "You like music?"

"I do, yeah. Johnny Mills sings songs like the way I want a relationship to be," she says, a look of surprise in her eyes. "What do you listen to?"

"Oh, I'm not picky. Whatever's on the radio or jukebox is enough for me."

Shelly visibly relaxes. The knowledge that she's not going to bolt tugs at something deep inside me. An overwhelming need to protect her, to be the one she can rely on, crashes over me. Still, I wish I could kick all the other guys out so she feels more comfortable. As it is, it's a Tuesday, and this is as quiet as the place gets.

"Balance your weight across both your feet and keep your back straight. Gloves under your chin." I hold my gloves up so she can see.

Shelly does the same. Her eyes are intent and focused as she watches, mimicking me as I show her the basics of moving her body and punching the bag.

"I think I'm getting the hang of this!" Excitement creeps into her voice as she finishes a repetition without making a mistake.

"Good job. Let's try it for real now. See this here?" I step over to the bag, which has a long line of masking tape down its length. When she nods, I continue. "Good. This is the center of the bag. That's where you aim. Got that?"

Shelly nods, bouncing on the balls of her feet. She says she hates fighting, but I recognize the energy building in her and needing to escape. It's obvious she's been holding a lot in and is finally somewhere she can let it out. It's amping her up. That's how it was for me the first time I walked into a gym and put on gloves.

"Okay, let's keep going." I stand in front of the heavy bag, making the same movements so she can keep the same pacing and not move too fast. Last thing she needs is to get injured.

"Step forward, punch out, step back," Shelly mutters under her breath, only faltering when she mistimes the bag's movement, and it swings too close for her to extend her arm fully.

"You're looking good, Shelly. Take your time and practice getting your form right. Getting sloppy will get you hurt. Remember to move your torso and put your upper body into the punch. Imagine your hand continuing to move after you make contact. You'll jam your hand up if you freeze when you make contact." I walk behind her and lightly touch her body, trying to ignore the seductive heat rolling off her skin. She flinches momentarily, then relaxes, letting me gently guide the movement of her body.

When Shelly begins to practice again, I notice a couple of the boxers watching her. I glare at them and discreetly shake my head. Shelly's off-limits. Fuck, I should be ignoring how attractive she is and how the air between us charges when we're standing close.

Mentally shaking my head to clear my thoughts, I focus on her. Satisfied that she's internalizing the movements, I instruct her to switch sides, reminding her that when punching with her right hand, she has to pivot her body into the punch.

Shelly falters a couple of times but catches her breath and keeps practicing until the pattern becomes easier. I stand behind her to assess her form, then catch myself staring at her thick hips as she steps forward and back.

Fuck. I could spend a lifetime holding onto those hips and making her scream in pleasure.

Whoa. I shake my head. She should be off limits, but I can't stop how my body reacts to her. I yearn to have her in my arms and whisper sweet nothings in her ear, but I know that's out of line. She's got some heavy shit to deal with. Besides, why would she want to date a boxer after surviving an abusive ex-boyfriend?

"What was up with you and that chick today?" Mannie asks, lifting his beer bottle and chugging it in one gulp before slamming it back on the bar and shaking his head like a wet dog. "Damn, I needed that. Champ was riding my ass like a motherfucker today."

"If you don't stop telegraphing all your moves, you'll be knocked out in the first round next weekend," I tell Mannie, who's young and excitable. He has talent but tries to move too fast with everything. "And Shelly is off limits."

I catch the bartender's attention and motion for new beers. He nods, grabs a couple of cold ones from the cooler, and slides them in front of us.

"Says who? I saw you looking at her," Mannie says with a challenge in his eyes.

I take a deep breath and steady myself. "She's got shit going on in her life. And yeah, she's an attractive woman," I say, downplaying the deep pull of desire I felt when I was with her. "She's skittish, and I've seen how you steamroll people—especially women—so don't go trying that shit with her."

Mannie looks at me as he grabs a fresh beer. "Dude, if you want first dibs on her, say it. If you wanna tap that ass, I ain't gonna cockblock you, but you gotta say if you're interested in her."

It's hard to say why Mannie talking like this bothers me so much, but it does. It's not like I didn't talk about women the same way when I was younger, though it's been a long time since I dated. My life hasn't been easy, and it's been easier to keep my own counsel after a certain point. It's not that I haven't wanted someone in my life, but after years of trying and failing to find a woman who knocked me out, you start to accept that maybe your destiny is to be a solitary man.

But Shelly took me by surprise. She was scared but fierce. There's a fire in her I want to fly closer to. I've seen a lot of hurt people in my time, but I've never felt the emotional pull that I do with her. I want to teach her how to protect herself, and I want her to trust me. It doesn't hurt that she's sexy as fuck, and if I let myself think about her, I'll be hard as a fucking rock.

"We'll see. But Mannie—whatever happens, she chooses it. She's not some prize for who gets there first or any of that shit. You gotta respect women if you want them to stick around." Protective anger rises in me. Shelly is more than a piece of meat. She's worth far more than a notch on a bedpost. Fuck. I don't even know her, but every atom of my body screams that I need her.

Mannie's laugh is brash and loud, almost louder than the music in The Roadhouse. "Relax, man. Relax. You want her, she's yours. As for me, I'll stop chasing all the beautiful women when I find one who's worth settling down with."

"There aren't that many women in this city, Mannie. You know that, right?" I laugh, relieved that Mannie isn't going to be a dick about this. "Raytown isn't the smallest town I've ever seen, but it sure isn't some metropolis like Los Angeles or New York."

"Yeah, we'll see what happens if this town runs out of women." He guzzles his beer, slams the bottle on the bar, and belches. "But for now, let's see what women are here tonight! The county fair is coming up, and I want a date. You saw that Johnny Mills is playing, right? Chicks dig that dude."

"Man, I don't like crowds like that. I wasn't planning on going. But maybe." I turn away from the bar and see the crowd gearing up for a rowdy night, but I'm not feeling it. All I want to do is think about the next time I'll see Shelly and her sexy body. Other boxers like skinny ring girls, but Shelly has some meat on her bones, and that makes her hotter than any of those ring girls. A woman who's always hungry or picking at salads isn't sexy. "Look, I'm gonna head out. I'll see you at the gym."

"You need to get laid, Floyd. You're so serious all the time."

I laugh. "Maybe so." There's only one woman I want.

My mind starts spinning as I hit the sidewalk and start my short walk home. If Johnny Mills is playing, then come hell or high water, I'm taking Shelly.

CHAPTER 3

SHELLY

I'm glad you finally made it to Champ's Gym. How was it?" My sister sits on my couch, hands me a bottle of beer, then opens a bottle of juice for herself.

"It was good, thanks." I take a sip from my beer. "Yeah...it was pretty tough, but it was okay once I was doing it. I'm not sure I'll ever get in a ring, but it was okay with the heavy bag."

She gives me a look, and I know she's biting her tongue. I've never seen two people happier than her and Caleb. She doesn't mind that he's a boxer, but...it's still hard for me to grasp why two people want to try and knock each other out. Though, I consider, maybe I'd feel differently if Larry hadn't knocked me around when he was angry or drunk.

"You'll see that it's not all bad. It can look scary, though. I was a nervous wreck when the first time I saw Caleb's fight. But the more I watch, the more I get it. But I understand why you wouldn't like it."

"Hm. Not sure I want to go to a fight, but I'll take your word for it." I smile.

Lu is the most supportive person in my life. I can't believe she almost moved away, but I knew she'd do it if that's what she wanted. We've always had different goals in life. I assumed I'd get married, have kids, and be a stay-at-home mom. Luann's always been ambitious and determined to make something of herself. I wasn't surprised when she said she was going to be a traveling nurse. I was so proud. It sounds silly, but I'm jealous of her life. I want the kind of love she's found with Caleb.

"What did you think of Floyd?" Lu asks carefully. He and Caleb are buddies, and she's met him several times.

"Floyd? Yeah, it was fine." I pause as the memory of him fills me with a sense of longing. He treated me respectfully, not like I was a victim or a ditz. I loved how he was patient with me like there was nothing else in the world he had to do. His steady calmness comforted me, especially since being in a boxing gym had me on edge.

I've never felt that way with anyone else. Everything was always unsteady with Larry. One day he'd treat me like a queen, and the next, he'd act like I was a drain on his soul. He made me believe I had to be perfect for him to treat me well.

"Just fine? Shelly Morgan, I've never heard you describe a man in so few words unless you felt the spark of desire." Lu's eyes glint with amusement as she sips her juice. "Fess up!"

I roll my eyes. "Lu, no. I'm not getting involved with anyone else for a while." I sigh, looking around my apartment. A box sits in the corner with the last of Larry's things. Everything here reminds me of him and our broken relationship. "Though, yes, he was certainly nice to look at."

"Wouldn't it be funny if we both settled down with boxers?" Lu asks, rubbing her pregnant belly and smiling.

"Yeah, I'm not sure about that. Besides, I'm not even sure Larry fully understands or accepts that I've ended things." I cringe, worrying about the next time I see him and his explosive temper when he finds out I meant it when I said I never wanted to see him again. "What guy would want to date me right now? My life is a mess." I sigh.

"What else is going on? Is everything okay?"

I take another drink of my beer and curl into my corner of the couch. "Nothing bad has happened. I've decided to get an Associate's degree at the community college, but my boss won't work with me on hours. It's not like I have promotion opportunities at the dealership, and I don't want to sell cars. I also want to move into a new apartment and start fresh, you know? I don't want the ghost of Larry haunting me."

Lu nods. "That's a lot to handle. You like your job, though, right?"

"Yeah, I like working in an office, for now anyway. I don't want to do it forever, which is why I want to go back to school. I want to take some classes and see what's interesting to me and what my options are. For now, I just wish I could find something like this that's part-time and flexible for me to take classes."

Lu is quiet for a moment before smiling at me. "I might know where you can get a job like that, though I'm not sure you'll like it."

"I'll consider anything that will get me a new apartment and into college." I look at my sister, excitement threading through me.

"Well, it's at Champ's. Since his sister got her job at the bank, he needs someone to help in the office."

"He needs an admin?" I ask, uncertain.

Luann's right—it's not my ideal work location, but maybe I could get used to it. At the very least, Larry wouldn't show up at my job. He did that once at the car dealership, and I nearly got fired because of the scene he made.

"I know it's bookkeeping, but there might be more to it. Basically, he needs someone to deal with the office and paperwork. Do you think you might be interested?"

I think about it and realize it's probably better than the car dealership. "I guess I should talk to him," I say hesitantly. "It might be weird to work there, but maybe it could work out okay."

I'm not sure if it's a good idea, but if he's willing to work with my schedule, it would be a hard offer to refuse. This isn't a tiny town, but it's not like there are *that* many options available.

"Oh, before I forget!" Lu's voice raises in excitement. "Did you see Johnny Mills is coming to the fair? Are you going? I know how much you love him. I know he was down and out for a while, but his new album has been at Number 1 for weeks now."

I sigh, looking away from my sister. "I wasn't planning on it. Larry liked his music too, and I sure as hell don't want to run into him on my own."

The excitement leaves my sister's voice. "Ugh. Is he in town? Or still on the road?"

"I don't know. I haven't heard from him since the last time I saw him, though I know he's going to try and weasel his way back into my life. He was never one to call me much while he was driving his rig unless he was checking up on me."

"Hm. I'd go with you, but I'm too pregnant. I could get Caleb to go with you," Lu offers.

That doesn't feel right. Johnny Mills' songs are romantic, and I can't imagine going with a man who isn't my boyfriend or someone I wanted to be my boyfriend.

"I'll pass. Thanks, though."

After we finish our visit, I lean back in my chair, wishing I could go to the concert. But fairs and concerts are never fun without friends or a boyfriend. It hurts that I'm making decisions about whether or not Larry will be in town, but I suppose it'll be a while before it's safe for me to do whatever I want.

I HEAD STRAIGHT to Champ's gym, having called ahead to make sure he's available. "Hey, Champ. Can we talk? "

He motions me over. "Come on. Let's go somewhere quiet."

"So, I was wondering if I could work here. As an admin, I mean. Luann said you needed some help in the office since Beth left."

Champ looks at me curiously. "And you want to do that?"

"Yes! I have admin experience. I'm looking for something part-time. I want to go to college and get a degree, but I'm working at the dealership now and they won't let me go down to part-time. I want to be able to go to classes in person, so I need something flexible."

Champ nods, thinking. "We might be able to work something out."

"Do you have any other references?" he asks, nodding as he reads.

"You could call the dealership. I've been there two years now." I cross my fingers behind my back. The dealership is the only job I've been an admin at. Everything else was part-time jobs like being a cashier at the grocery store or waiting tables at the chain restaurant out by the freeway.

"Okay, let me think about it and we'll talk later." Champ looks at me thoughtfully, but doesn't say anything further. One of the guys in the gym hollers his name and he raises his hand. "Mannie needs me, but you and I can probably make it work. I'll get back to you soon."

"Thanks, Champ. I appreciate it." Relief floods through me. This would make my life so much easier. I've been dreading trying to find a job that would work with my hours, and I haven't wanted to go back to the grocery store or waiting tables.

On the drive home, I wonder if potentially working in a boxing gym is a good idea. But so far, Caleb, Champ, and Floyd have been down-to-earth guys and not assholes, so it seems like it would be an okay job. It also wouldn't hurt to be able to see Floyd more often.

CHAPTER 4

FLOYD

As I walk into the gym and look around to see who's practicing and working out, Champ catches my eye and makes a beeline for me.

"Floyd, can we talk?" Champ's voice is tense. "In the office."

"What's up?" I ask, setting down my gear bag.

Champ closes the door firmly before turning to face me, his arms crossed over his chest. "I heard from Harley. There's a situation in Fresno." He takes a deep breath and exhales, but his muscles flex like he's aching to fight. If Harley is calling for help, the situation is bad. "You available to roll out if he asks for help?"

"Fuck. Yeah, I am. Leo will understand if I need to take a couple of days off. He's cool with what we do. Say the word, and I'll gas up the truck. You know my go bag is in my truck."

Champ exhales. "Thanks, man. I'll keep you posted. Harley's trying to handle it on his own, but you know that damn man thinks he's an army of one."

I chuckle and nod. "Yeah, you've told me about the times you've had to bail him out. We need to make sure he stays in business."

"You got that right. Okay, now that's out of the way, there's something else."

I watch Champ. I haven't been here long, but we both know Harley, which created an instant bond between us. Harley has a vast network, and if you're in it, you're family.

"This girl, Shelly. You like her?"

The question startles me. "How do you mean?" While I barely know her, I know I want her in my life, but that's not something I'm planning to blab all over the place.

"Luann told Shelly I needed someone part-time here in the office, and Shelly came to talk to me about it. She seems to have her head on straight, and I'd rather have someone in here who's been vouched for. You cool with that?"

"Why wouldn't I be?"

"Floyd, man, I'm not blind. I saw how you two were the other day. I've never seen you that patient with anyone in this gym, and I saw how she looked at you." Champ chuckles as he looks at me.

"Shelly," I pause, exhaling and choosing my words carefully. "Is she an attractive woman? Fuck, yeah, she is. But she also has baggage, so anything that happens is on her terms. *If* anything happens. I'm considering asking her out to the fair, but we'll see."

"So you okay if she's here in the office?" Champ looks at me carefully. The man is always ready to do anything for his family, whether blood or through his network here at the gym or beyond, but otherwise, he has a low tolerance for drama. He always says he'll get in the ring if he wants a fight.

I think for a moment and nod. "Yeah, no reason not to be."

"Good to know. But you gotta vow that if she says no to you, or you go out and it doesn't work, you'll respect her. She can't be uncomfortable here. You'll have to answer to me if that happens. You got that?"

"Yeah, Champ. I do." I may not have been here long, but Champ's Gym already feels like home and family. I'm not going to jeopardize my place here.

I SWEAR, every time the front door opens and slams shut, I glance over to see if it's Shelly.

The moment Shelly *does* walk in, my heart pounds. Inwardly, I pump my fist at how happy I am to see her. Every atom of my body is firing on high alert, and I'm aching to be with her.

"Hey. How's it going?" I ask, trying to temper my excitement. I'm not sure I've ever wanted to see someone as much as I've wanted to see her. It's been a week since she was in here, and every minute without seeing her has been excruciating.

"Good." She smiles and slips off her jacket. "I'm starting to get used to this place."

"This is only your second time here, though. Right?"

"Well," she looks at me shyly, her big blue eyes tender. "I'm still not sure about the actual fighting, but I know Caleb, and now you and Champ. It feels a little safer and a lot less like walking into something dangerous. Does that make sense?"

Hearing that I make her feel safe fills me with unshakable pride. "It does, yes. A lot of things are less scary once you experience or understand them."

"I gotta admit, I've been looking forward to our session today." Her voice is quiet but earnest, and I see a flicker of the attraction I hoped would be reciprocated.

"Me, too." I wink at her, letting my hand rest on her shoulder. She doesn't flinch or look at my hand, and we share a moment where me touching her is the most natural thing in the world. "Another band?" I nod at her t-shirt.

"Do you know them?" Shelly's voice rises in excitement.

"I don't. What are they like? But tell me as you warm up."

Shelly describes their music as she practices with the heavy bag. A lot rock and roll, a little country, a little blues. "They're great to dance to. Do you dance?"

I chuckle and shake my head. "Not really, Shelly. The only dancing I do is in the ring. I'd be open to learning sometime."

"That could be arranged." Shelly smiles at me, her eyes lit up with happiness.

A punch of desire lights up my soul. I don't know much about music beyond listening to whatever's on the radio in my truck or at the bar, and I don't know how to dance, but damn if she doesn't make me want to learn about both. Something tells me that dancing with her in my arms would feel better than winning the lottery.

I swear I never thought I'd want a woman in my life, but there's a glow about Shelly that makes me unable to look away from her.

Like most of the guys I know, my life had a hard start. My parents didn't fight like so many of my friends' parents, but everything was tough, and we were scraping by to survive. Early on, I learned how to fight for what I wanted, but my mom was tough, made me stay in school, and did her damnedest to keep me off the streets. When she figured out I had a talent for boxing, she got an extra job on the weekends to pay for classes and equipment.

Watching Shelly go through the motions, her eyes bright with the happiness of discovering something she likes and is good at, reminds me of when I learned how to box. Discovering I was good at something gave me a reason to fight for more than the down-and-out life I'd grown up expecting to have. Seeing Shelly like this shows she's not willing to accept the status quo but wants to fight for something better than what she has. I respect the fuck out of that.

I watch with pride as she goes through the moves and punches I showed her last time. She's clearly practiced since I last saw her. Having a committed student makes me proud not just because she's learning, but also because she'll be able to protect herself if the need arises.

"Good job back there," I say, handing her a cool bottle of water. My heart speeds up when she lets her fingers linger against mine for a moment and looks me in the eye, a smile on her lips. "You're doing well."

"Thanks." She flushes with pride as she unscrews the bottle cap. She tilts the bottle and takes a long drink, and I stare longingly at her pale throat, wanting to cover it in kisses. "You're a good teacher."

Her compliment takes me by surprise, and my cheeks warm. As she's about to walk away for the day, I reach out and lightly touch her arm. "Shelly?"

She turns to me, her eyes filled with an eagerness that makes my heart pound. "Yes?"

"Would you like to go to the fair with me this weekend? That band whose t-shirt you were wearing last week is playing at the fair Saturday night. I thought you might enjoy going."

Shelly is quiet for a long moment, and fear spikes through me. Did I go too far? Dammit. If I've fucked this up, I'll never forgive myself.

"You're the second person to mention the fair to me." Shelly smiles, and her blue eyes twinkle. "For you, I'll say yes. I'd love to go to the fair with you. I might even teach you how to dance."

This woman is stealing my heart.

CHAPTER 5

SHELLY

The lights and noise of the fair and the smell of cotton candy and caramel popcorn immerse me in memories of being a kid before life got complicated and messy.

"Thank you for inviting me here tonight, Floyd." I reach out and touch his arm, my emotions warming when I see the way he smiles at me. His smile is filled with contentment. I don't feel I have to be anyone other than who I am.

"It's my pleasure that you agreed to come tonight and introduce me to Johnny Mills."

"Did you like him? It's been years since I saw him perform live, and seeing him tonight made me realize I need to go to live music more often. It makes me feel alive!"

Floyd chuckles, and my skin warms as his hand on my lower back as he guides me through the crowd, like he has to have contact with me to ensure he doesn't lose me. I swore I wouldn't date anyone for a long time, but Floyd is everything I've ever wanted in a man. It's obvious there's an attraction that pulls us together, but can that attraction withstand the utter trainwreck that my life is right now?

"I enjoyed the music, yes," Floyd says, though I'm unconvinced.

"Do you even like music?" I ask, stopping before a game booth that involves throwing a baseball at painted bottles. "Win me a stuffed animal?" I give Floyd my biggest smile and laugh as I bat my eyelashes at him. Miraculously, he laughs and nods. He seems willing to do anything to make me happy.

"Three balls," he says, slapping cash on the dusty counter. In quick succession, he throws the balls, and three bottles are knocked over in a line.

"Did you play baseball?" I would never have imagined he'd have an aim like that. Sure, I want the teddy bear the kid behind the counter hands me, but I didn't realize Floyd would win it so quickly.

"No more than the next guy in school. Just got good aim, I guess."

I sense there's something he's not saying, but I let it pass. If I'm reading everything right, we have a long time ahead of us to get to know the little details of each other's life and childhood.

It feels juvenile to be so happy over a cheap stuffed animal, but it's been a long time since a man has wanted to make me happy, and I need something to remind me of this night. In the middle of the chaos that is the county fair, Floyd and I exist in a bubble that sparkles with the possibility of what we might be together. I couldn't imagine a more perfect Saturday night.

"Hey, I was meaning to talk to you about something. Champ offered me a job in the office at the gym. Is it going to be weird if I'm working there?"

"Seeing you more often will make me happy. That's the God's honest truth." Floyd takes my hand and gently kisses my knuckles, then the palm of my hand. "I want you in my life, Shelly. More than as my student."

"Why? I mean, don't get me wrong. I'm having a real good time with you tonight, and I like you, but my life is so messed up right now. My ex will probably come round again, whether I want it or not—and obviously, I do not."

"Waiting for a perfect time is a fool's game, Shelly. You're working to make your life what you want it to be. Include me in that." Floyd's eyes hold a vulnerability. "I'll stand by you and give you all the support I can. I know about striving for more than you come from because that's what I did. Let me be here to catch you when you need it or guide you if you want that. I care about you, Shelly."

Floyd's eyes are open and honest, and my heart knows I can trust him. A warm contentment fills me, and I give him a quick hug. He laces his fingers through mine, and the flush of hope from holding hands with a hot man for the first time makes me happier than I've been in a long time.

"Can we talk about this more later?" My heart is already telling me to say yes, but as nice as Floyd has been, my head is telling me to slow down.

"Of course. I'm not going anywhere."

We walk in silence for a little, enjoying the fair and dodging groups of amped-up teenagers.

"Are you hungry? You were sure dancing a lot at the concert–" Floyd stops talking, and when I follow his gaze and see why, my heart drops. By the look Larry is giving us, Floyd can guess who he is.

"I might've known I'd find you here."

The blood drains from my face as Larry speaks. *Please, God. I was having such a good night!* He's standing a few feet from us, a couple of friends at his side.

"What are you doing here?" I challenge him. I will myself not to shrink like I always did when he was around. I remind myself I broke it off with him, even if he doesn't want to remember that.

"Now that I've found you, it's time we go home." He glances at Floyd, sizing him up but ignoring him.

"I don't think so." I cross my arms over my chest, openly defying him for maybe the first time. Confidence and power surge up in me. *How in the hell did I put up with this for so long?*

Larry's friends look at each other and chuckle. They probably expect Larry and Floyd to start fighting, which I wouldn't put past either of them. I'm close enough to Floyd to hear his breathing change and feel his body tense.

"Don't make a scene," Larry continues, softening his voice like there's nothing wrong. "I don't need no one thinking I can't control my woman."

I close my eyes for a long moment, trying to push down the anger rising in me. My fingernails cut into the palms of my hands as I clench my hands into fists.

This isn't who you are, Shelly. Calm down, and don't take the bait.

I stand my ground. "I'm not going anywhere with you, Larry. Now or ever. You need to get that through your thick skull. I am not your woman."

Floyd puts his hand on my back, and a rush of security floods through me. I know that with Floyd here, Larry won't be able to do anything to me.

His friends laugh as I glare at Larry.

"I said," he growls, "come here."

"And I said no. You can't make me go with you."

Larry's face burns red with anger, and he flicks his eyes toward Floyd again, clearly wondering if he can take him. Larry steps in front of me, and his fingers claw into my arm. I wince at the familiarity of the pain he inflicts.

"Let go of me!" I yell, struggling to get away. Alarm races through me. Did I just make a huge mistake? Is tonight going to end up with someone in the ER?

"Do as Shelly asks, Larry." Floyd says, his voice firm and steady. "She's not going anywhere with you."

"And who the fuck do you think you are?" Larry demands, shifting his attention to Floyd. His lips form into a sneer. "Or do you like the fat ones, too? The ones who'll do anything you want and keep you warm at night?"

"I'm with Floyd, Larry, not you." I look Larry in the eyes, my voice filled with defiance.

It takes every bit of strength I've ever had to ignore his comments about my weight and the implication I'll do anything just because he thinks I'm desperate. There was a time when I had feelings for him and thought he had feelings for me, too. It's not like he advertised that he was an abuser.

I don't have to do what he wants. Not anymore.

"I'm not gonna repeat myself," Floyd warns, his voice thick with restrained anger. "Let go of Shelly."

Floyd standing up to Larry is like a red rag to a bull. He loosens his grip on my arm as he shifts his attention to Floyd. With my other hand, I push him away, and he returns his attention to me.

"Don't think you can get away from me. I'm not done with you," Larry threatens. "I mean it."

His face falls into the familiar promise of punishment he gets when he's mad. But for once, I'm not letting my fear make me weak. Even if Floyd wasn't with me, my resolve for a better life for myself is stronger than my fear of Larry when he gets like this.

A red mist descends in front of my eyes, and before I'm conscious of what I'm doing, I'm changing my stance, lifting my hands, and then pulling my right arm back. My fist and arm move rapidly through the air as I twist my body, and my fist collides with Larry's face.

Larry grunts as his head snaps to the side, and he falls over on the dusty dirt of the fairground, knocked out cold.

"Ow!" I scream, bending over and cradling my hand.

I never realized that hitting somebody would hurt so much. The sound of a group of girls cheering me on suddenly reminds me that people are watching me and have just seen me punch a man.

Oh, God. What must they think of me? Is she making a video?

For a hot moment, shame fills me that I resorted to violence, but when one of the women walks by me, she smiles and says, "You go, girl. Fucking asshole deserved it. I had a guy like that once and kicking his sorry ass to the curb is the best thing I ever did."

I look at her, my brain scrambled, before turning back to Floyd. What did I just do?

"You take this piece of shit here and leave now before this gets worse," Floyd warns Larry's friends.

They look from us to Larry lying still on the ground, his eyes starting to flutter open. Floyd wraps an arm around me possessively and stares down at Larry. Amazement fills me as Larry's friends lift him and walk him away from us. I watch them in shock.

I did that. I did that!

Fear crashes into me when I see them stop walking, and Larry turns back to me. He stares at me with impotent rage, and I know this isn't the end of it. He opens his mouth as if to say something but then closes it and walks away.

My breathing comes out jagged as adrenaline and relief flood through me, and I realize I've knocked Larry out.

"Are you okay, Shelly?" Floyd asks, angling his body so he's facing me.

His voice is quiet and reassuring, which is good because I'm about to start sobbing with all the emotions raging through me. I just hit somebody in anger.

My voice trembles, and I cling to Floyd. "Take me away from here, Floyd. I need to get away."

CHAPTER 6

FLOYD

"Hey, sweetheart. You doing okay?"

We've pulled up at a stoplight a mile from my place. Shelly's been quiet the whole drive, but she's trembling as tears slip down her face.

"I don't know." Shelly hesitates, her eyes filled with so much raw emotion that it shakes my core with anger.

Fuck Larry for ruining my date with Shelly. I wanted to punch him myself, though I knew that wouldn't make Shelly happy, and it wasn't my fight. Still, I damn well wanted to put that bastard in his place. Watching a woman cry is one of my least favorite things, but wanting to dole out punishment to a man who makes a woman cry? That's something else entirely.

It was so unexpected when Shelly punched him, but damn if I wasn't proud of her. Her punch was perfect, and she knocked that son of a bitch right out. She's *my* knockout, that's for damn sure.

"We're almost home," I say, reaching out and rubbing her arm. She clings to the stuffed bear I won for her like it's the only thing keeping her from losing it.

After I park and go to help Shelly out of my truck, she collapses into my arms. All the emotion she's been trying to hold back comes rushing out of her. Her body is wracked with sobs, and she mutters under her breath.

"Come here, Shelly. Shhh. It's okay. You're safe now."

Shelly lets me take her in my arms and clings to me as she cries out her emotions. Nothing could make me move from this spot. All I want is to protect her and give her anything she needs. If I knew it wouldn't alienate her, I'd take care of Larry myself in a permanent way. I know some guys up on King Mountain who can make certain problems disappear without a trace up there in the woods.

Eventually, Shelly's breathing evens out, and her heartbeat calms down. I run my hand over her head, stroking the dark curls of her silky hair.

"Thank you, Floyd." Shelly looks up at me, her eyes red and swollen.

I lean forward and kiss her forehead. "No thanks are needed. You did well at taking care of him yourself." I smile at her, pride welling up in me again. There's no denying that I'm happy to have helped her learn how to protect herself. I know this isn't over, but I also know that we'll get through it.

"I must look terrible," she says, rubbing her hands over her face.

"Shelly, stop apologizing. You've been through a difficult experience. You stood up for yourself and were amazing."

She looks at me, considering what I've said. "But I hit someone, Floyd. You understand how much I hate violence, right?" Her lip trembles, and a fresh round of tears start.

"I do, Shelly. But," I hesitate, unsure how to say what I want and not push her away. "When you're dealing with weak men or bullies, sometimes it's unavoidable. I know that's not what you want to hear, but it's the truth."

"Maybe." Shelly gulps air and rubs her eyes. "I hate myself for hitting him, though. It's not like he didn't deserve it, but it's hard to reconcile, you know?"

"I understand. Maybe think of it differently?" I give her a moment to think about this, then continue. "You've said you want to take control of your life so you can move forward in a way that satisfies you."

"Yes, that's right."

"Alright. Change is hard, and sometimes it's painful. Just because you punched Larry–and you're right that he deserved it–that doesn't mean you're going to start hitting everyone who upsets you. He was trying to hurt you, and you defended yourself. You're not a bad person. It's as simple as that."

"I'm still appalled at my behavior." Shelly looks ready to cry again.

I take her hands in mine and look into her blue eyes. "It's okay to feel guilty about it. I'll tell you something else–I'm proud of you, Shelly. You stood up for yourself, and you threw a perfect fucking punch. You're a good student."

Shelly chuckles, and her tension eases slightly. "Yeah, well, I have a good teacher. I'm not sure what I would've done if you hadn't been there."

"You would've been fine. You're strong and brave, and you're learning how to defend yourself. Never apologize for that."

The smile on Shelly's face is so broad and genuine that love surges through me. I know there's so much more to learn about her, but dammit, Shelly has knocked me sideways. She's tender and fierce and willing to do what's necessary to make her life better.

"How's your hand?"

Shelly looks at it as if just noticing that her knuckles are red and her hand is swollen. "It's stiff and hurts, but I don't think I need to go to the hospital." She wiggles her fingers and winces, but nothing is broken.

"You got him pretty good." I stand from my couch. "Come with me. I'll get you some ibuprofen and a bag of peas so you can ice your hand and minimize the swelling."

I take Shelly into the kitchen, grabbing a clean towel and a bag of frozen peas. "Here. Go back to the couch and put this on your hand. I'll get some ibuprofen for the pain and the swelling."

When I rejoin Shelly in the living room, I hand her the pills and a glass of water. She takes them and leans back.

"Thank you," she whispers, her voice thick with emotion.

"It's going to hurt for a few days. No hitting anything. You need something hit, you call me, and I'll do it."

She chuckles, reaching up to touch my face, her fingers stroking my beard. "Thank you. You let me stand up for myself. Men have always tried to do everything for me. I like that you let me be me. I know you're here for me. I value you."

"I'll always be here for you, Shelly. Always." I carefully wrap my hands over hers, ensuring the ice pack doesn't slip. "Are you feeling better now?"

I take a deep breath. My heartbeat races because it's impossible to deny how attracted I am to Shelly when we're close and alone like this.

"A little. Being with you helps." Shelly smiles, and I know everything will be okay.

"Good." I pause, and the air between us feels heavy with so many conversations we haven't yet had. "Shelly, I'm just going to say it. I like you—a lot. I want you in my life as more than a woman I'm teaching self-defense to."

"Oh, Floyd," Shelly says, her voice catching. "I like you, too, but are you sure? My life is a mess. You saw Larry. He's not going to give up on me that easy."

"Then he'll have me, and everyone else at the gym, to deal with."

"I don't even know what's going on with my life."

"We can figure it out together," I say, filled with determination. "I want to be with you, Shelly. Now I've found you, I'm not letting you get away."

CHAPTER 7

SHELLY

"I'm serious, Shelly," Floyd says, reaching up and cradling my face in his hands. "I'm not going anywhere unless you tell me to. You're a knockout, and there isn't a doubt in my mind that I want to spend my life with you."

"Oh, Floyd." My eyes glisten with tears as I run my hand over his short, dark hair. I knew I liked him the moment I saw him, but I never imagined anything like this would happen.

"I haven't forgotten that you said you wanted to be single," Floyd says, his voice nearly choking. "So if I have to wait for you, I'll wait. I'll give you all the space you need."

I'm blindsided by all the emotions rising in me. There's no doubt in my heart that I care deeply for this man. Am I being disloyal to myself if I start seeing him?

No, Shelly. You're only disloyal if you compromise.

"Be honest, Floyd. Why did you ask me to the fair and to see Johnny Mills?"

"Because it was obvious you like music, and you were wearing a t-shirt from one of his concerts. I wanted to do something with you that you like. I thought it'd be a way to get to know you better."

I'm sure my mouth must be hanging open because I'm stunned. Going to see a band because I liked them isn't something Larry would have even considered. I blink quickly, reminding myself not to compare Floyd to Larry because they're nothing alike.

Floyd goes out of his way to treat me with respect and shows that he cares about me, not how he thinks I might fit in with what he wants. He's everything I've wanted in a man.

I smile. "Would you learn how to dance if I asked?"

Floyd responds in an instant. "Are you saying you'd like to spend more time in my arms? I'd learn any dance if it meant I could hold you."

He takes the frozen peas off my hand and tenderly checks my knuckles before lifting my hand to his mouth and placing a tender kiss on each bruised knuckle.

I smile at him as deep emotions run through me. Floyd returns my smile, and I can see the love in his eyes. I let out a breath of relief as I realize that I've finally met a man who loves and respects me for exactly the woman I am. As messed up as my life is, I can't let go of Floyd, and I need to give him a chance.

"Something like that, yes." As happy as I am, it feels strange to open myself up to a man so soon after ending things with Larry. Yet there isn't a drop of doubt in me about how much Floyd cares for me. I take a deep breath, knowing I'm exactly where I'm supposed to be. My heart swells with emotion, and I know I'm ready to take a chance on this amazing man. "You don't have to wait, because I want you, too."

I turn my head, and my mouth finds Floyd's. Our kiss starts gently, but he pulls me closer as our kiss becomes hungrier and more frantic. Each stroke of his tongue makes me moan with urgent desire. I run my hands over his chest, searching for the edge of his shirt so I can caress his bare skin.

Gasping as Floyd grazes his teeth over my neck, I find the bottom of his t-shirt and frantically pull it over his head. I bite my lip as I take in his chest, letting my fingertips trace over his skin. I grin when he flexes for me, showing off his muscular body.

"Let me see you." Floyd's voice is quiet and urgent as his eyes rake over my body. "I want to see all of the fiercest, most beautiful woman I've ever met."

A blush burns at my cheeks. I know my eyes are a mess from crying, but Floyd sees me as I am and as I want to be. It doesn't matter to him that my eye makeup is ruined and my eyes are red from crying. Having Floyd see me at…not my worst, but at not my best, and still wanting to be in my life? It causes my heart to expand with even more love for him. He's the kind of man I didn't think I'd find for myself.

For every piece of clothing Floyd takes off my body, he explores the revealed skin with his fingertips and mouth. Waves of pleasure ripple across my skin, and a passionate flame builds in my core. I'm more certain about Floyd than I've ever been about anyone or anything, and it takes my breath away.

"Let me make love to you." Floyd's voice is husky with desire as he looks at me, his eyes taking in every inch of my curvy body. He caresses my skin as if I'm the most precious thing in the world and makes me feel beautiful and sexy.

"Let's make love together." I reach up and stroke Floyd's beard, trailing my hands down his arms and lacing my fingers through his.

When he squeezes my fingers tightly and guides me to his bedroom, my world shifts, and I know everything about Floyd is right.

We fall into his bed, giggling as we move closer and tease each other with tickles and kisses. Floyd moves his body over mine, and my core sings out with the need for Floyd to enter me and move with my body. He slides his hard cock through my slick folds, teasing me, and my body shivers with anticipation.

"Please, Floyd," I moan, wrapping my arms around his torso and trying to pull him down to me.

"I like watching you squirm like this," he teases, resisting me as I pull him down.

He lowers his head and takes the peak of my breast between his lips, sucking my straining nipple and making me cry out from the delicious pleasure of his tongue roughly flicking over my hyper-sensitive skin.

His cock bumps against my throbbing core, and I push my hips up to meet him. We both moan as he slides inside me.

"Oh my God," I cry out.

My body is on fire with the sensation of Floyd inside me. Each stroke sets off a series of bright explosions of pleasure in my body. He moves slowly, drawing out each thrust excruciatingly and making my body yearn for the release of ecstasy I know is coming.

Floyd lowers his mouth to mine, and our kiss is deep and electric, our tongues dancing as we join our souls. He begins thrusting faster and deeper inside me, and I moan into his mouth. I raise my hips against him as he moves deep inside me, his perfect cock rubbing against my G-spot like he was made specifically for me. Electric bursts of desire radiate from my core, and I know I won't last much longer. My emotions crash over me, building on the pleasure Floyd is bringing me.

"I'm starting to come!" My body bucks and grinds against Floyd's, each stroke unlocking my pleasure.

Stars flash in front of my eyes as my orgasm explodes through my body, making me pant and pull Floyd closer to me. As my pleasure bursts over me, our profound connection engulfs me. We barely know the details about each other, but my heart and soul understand the kind of man he is, and there's no doubt in my mind that I love him.

Floyd is still above me, his wild eyes watching me. "I love my knockout," he says, his cock plunging deep inside me, faster and faster, as his body shakes and his breathing comes in sharp gasps. He stills as he comes, and his eyelids flutter as he moans my name.

"That was amazing," I say, pulling Floyd close and relishing his skin against mine.

His heart pounds as he catches his breath, his eyes locked with mine. "Only amazing, my knockout?" he asks, kissing me slowly and tenderly.

Tenderness fills my eyes as I share this moment with him. I know that nothing and no one will ever come between us. Floyd doesn't just flatter or praise me, but he also stands beside me and lifts me up, even when things are difficult.

"Okay, maybe a little better than amazing," I tease. "I may need to do a little more research. For educational purposes, you know."

Floyd pulls me close against him, and I rest my head on his chest. "I love you, Shelly. More than I thought I'd ever love anyone."

"I love you, too, Floyd."

I push him onto his back and shift my body to straddle his hips. Satisfaction washes over me as he watches me rub my core against him. He's already hard again, and I can't wait to have him inside me so we can keep sharing this perfect pleasure.

"I'll never let you go, Shelly." Floyd gasps as he pushes up into me.

I let myself be me, giving myself over to a love I never imagined I'd find. Nothing could beat the perfection of this moment with Floyd. It's just the beginning of a lifetime of moments that will strengthen our love.

I've found my happy ending.

EPILOGUE

"Congratulations, Shelly. We're so proud of you!" My sister comes over to me and gives me a huge hug.

My cheeks hurt from smiling so much. Champ is hosting a huge barbecue down at the lake, to celebrate me finishing my first year at the community college. All of the guys from the gym are here, plus a lot of my friends.

"Thanks, Lu. And thank you again for setting me up with the job with Champ in the gym. I wouldn't have been able to go to college otherwise."

"I'm so glad it worked out for you. We're all also glad for Champ because we know how much help he needed." Daisy gurgles, and Lu picks up her daughter and bounces her. She never thought she'd be a mom, but watching them together is precious. She loves Daisy so much.

I laugh and look across the picnic area toward Champ, who's talking with Caleb, Dirk, and a couple of other boxers. They're having an animated conversation, and a couple of the guys are throwing fake punches at each other, which is about normal for them. They're always messing around, especially the younger boxers.

"Yeah." I nod, turning my attention back to her and my niece. "His books were a mess when I started. I thought it would just be a little bit of paying the bills and making sure the checking account was never overdrawn, but it was so much more than that. But I enjoy it, and it's helped me realize that studying business is what I want to focus on. It's amazing working for Champ."

Caleb joins us, kissing Lu on the cheek. He turns to Lu and holds out his arms. "Give Daisy to me. You can take a break."

Lu smiles as she hands him their daughter, then leans over to kiss him. "Thanks, handsome."

Caleb turns to me. "What's going on with you and the new gym? It seems like you're in both places a lot."

"I am, but I won't be able to juggle both gyms when I'm back in school in the fall. Beth introduced me to a friend of hers who's also in the business track at the community college. I'm working on buttering up Champ so he'll hire Opal for the second gym. She lives over in Jefferson anyway."

"Isn't Opal…?" Luan lets her question trail off, tilting her head at me. It's obvious Beth has told her who Opal is.

"Yeah, she is. But I will kill you if you tell Champ. He'll never give her a chance if he knows who she is." I give her a stern look. Lu isn't the biggest gossip in town, but Beth and I have a lot riding on this.

Caleb laughs and shifts Daisy from one hip to the other. "Champ might kill you if he finds out you're keeping secrets from him."

Even though I don't think Caleb knows who Opal is, I warn him, too. "Don't you say anything, either."

∼

AFTER MY SHOWDOWN with Larry at the county fair last year, a video of me knocking Larry out went viral. It took me a long time to get over the shame of a video of me punching him in the face and knocking him out being seen by so many people, but eventually, I forgave the stranger who'd recorded and uploaded the incident.

One good thing from the video was that Larry's and my faces were crystal clear. Everyone who's ever known him has watched him get knocked out by a woman. I haven't seen him since, but I've heard on the grapevine that he never mentions my name. As much as I hate what I did, it's worth it knowing Larry will never bother me again.

Since that viral video, a ton of women in the Heartland region now want boxing or self-defense classes, and they all want them at Champ's Gym. Champ tried to add a couple of classes to the main gym, but the demand was so high, especially from women over in Jefferson, he decided to open another gym and add self-defense classes there, too. It's getting off the ground, and Champ is working with a group of new boxers over there.

That's where I want Opal to come in. Champ is all about family. Even if it's found family. All his boxers and their families and friends are capital F family. I only need to convince him that Opal will do a good job and he can trust her, he'll let me hire her.

Beth and I have another plan we haven't told anybody about, not even our men. Our secret must be kept from Champ at all costs. If it works out, he'll thank us. But in the meantime, our lips are sealed.

~

"You did good, kid." Champ gives me a one-arm hug as we look at the other boxers and their families playing in the park as the barbecue winds down.

"Thank you, Champ, for everything. I wouldn't be here if it wasn't for you," I say sincerely, covering my eyes from the sun as I look up at him. Champ took a leap of faith when he hired me, and I'll never forget that.

"Oh, stop with that," he says, though I know he's proud of how much he was able to help me achieve my dreams of going to college.

One of the things I've learned about Champ is how much it means to him to champion other people and guide them on a better path in life. He just doesn't like it much when people make a big deal about it.

"I'm glad that you and Floyd still like each other because I'm not giving him up as an instructor, and I don't want to give you up in the office."

"You don't have to worry, Champ." I laugh. "Neither of us is going anywhere. You'll listen to me one of these days and hire another girl for the office, right, Champ?" I don't know why it's taken so long for him to admit he needs more help.

"We'll see about that," he says. "Surely you can take care of the books at both gyms."

I sigh. "Champ, we've had this conversation. I can't do the books for both gyms while I'm still in school. And you know how important it is for me to finish this degree. Once I finish my Associates next year, I want to transfer and do a four-year degree. Though I'll probably do that at an online university because I'm not leaving Raytown, and I'm not leaving Floyd."

Champ grunts and looks away, his forehead creased. He's one of the most hard-headed people I've ever met. Stubborn doesn't begin to cover it.

"Yeah, I suppose. Do you know someone who could help? I only want someone I can trust. No stranger is doing the books for my gym."

I smile. "Actually, Champ, I do."

∽

"Can I steal my beautiful fiancée from you?" Floyd asks, wrapping his arms around me from behind and kissing my neck. Feeling his body pressed against mine makes me long to get home, so we can get naked.

"Yeah, you two need to take that elsewhere," Champ says, but he laughs. "I'll leave you to it. I'll see you both on Monday."

Floyd takes my hand in his as we make our way to one of the picnic tables down by the lake and sit in the shade of a tree.

"Do you need anything to drink? Anything to eat?" Floyd asks.

He's so devoted and doting on me and I thank my stars every single day that our paths crossed.

"No, babe, I'm okay. I just want to spend time with my man." I press my leg against his, relishing the moment to ourselves.

"You know I can never say no to you, sweetheart. I'm so proud of you for all your hard work this year." Floyd puts his arm around my shoulders, and I lean into him, happiness filling every atom of my soul.

I've always dreamed of having a love like ours. We're deeply in love and incredibly supportive of each other, and there are never any games or doubts about his feelings for me. He just loves me. It's the most freeing thing to love him with abandon and be loved the same way in return. "Thank you for supporting me like you have. You're my rock. I love you, babe."

"I love you too, sweetheart. How are Luanne and Caleb doing? I haven't seen them much lately because Caleb has been over in Jefferson at the new gym. How's their baby?"

"The baby is beautiful. I love my niece. Luanne says she was boxing in her belly instead of kicking."

Floyd laughs. " That sounds about right. What do you expect from the child of a boxer? Even if it is a girl."

"*Even if it is a girl?*" I scold. "We can throw punches too."

"Don't I know it, my knockout." Floyd turns his head to mine and kisses me long and slow.

Familiar desire fills me, making me eager for the barbecue to wrap up so we can go home.

Nothing on this earth could separate Floyd and me. And I wouldn't have it any other way.

∽

Thank you so much for reading *Knockout*! If you enjoyed it, please leave a review on your favorite retailer, Goodreads, or Bookbub!

Your feedback helps other readers find my books and lets me know which books you like best!

Champion is the next book in the series! You can preorder Champ and Opal's story at:

https://www.amazon.com/dp/B0BTRY53WX

This book is part of the Heartland Heroes series. To catch up on the full series, please visit:

https://www.amazon.com/dp/B0BFRNY6CW

Want to stay up to date on new releases, sales, and freebies! Join my newsletter!

http://eepurl.com/dh59Xr

For more Lana Love books, please visit my Amazon page at:

https://www.amazon.com/Lana-Love/e/B078KKRB1T/

https://www.loveheartbooks.com

ABOUT LANA LOVE

Lana Love is a USA Today Bestselling Author of steamy stories about relatable women, and the strong men who will move heaven and earth to capture the heart of the curvy woman they can't live without. Curvy since forever, Lana writes the heroines she never read about or saw in movies when she was growing up.

Lana lives in the Pacific Northwest and is passionate about dancing, travel, chocolate, and cocktails, and writing stories that make her heart race and bring her fantasies to life. She loves a man who loves curves and who knows what to do with them!

For books with relatable women, sinfully hot men, and steam that will melt your e-reader, you've found a new favorite author!

https://www.loveheartbooks.com

You can follow me on social media at:

https://www.goodreads.com/author/show/12219675.Lana_Love

https://www.bookbub.com/profile/lana-love

https://www.facebook.com/groups/746330989530967

Printed in Great Britain
by Amazon